To Freya ~

Always remember, an[d]

can be a Snorkel [

Dawn S. Calisto

2017

The Snorkel Bunnies!

A Sea Turtle Adventure

by Dawn Stanford Calisto

Illustrated by Madalyn McLeod

Warren Publishing, Inc.

Published by Warren Publishing, Inc.
Charlotte, NC
www.warrenpublishing.net

ISBN: 978-1-943258-06-2
Library of Congress Control Number: 2016935144

Dedication

For Nicole, Morgan, Rachel and Sami, the original Snorkel Bunnies!
And to Joey, my husband and best friend. Thank you all for your
encouragement, support, incredible sense of humor and the joy you
bring! I couldn't love you more!

Have you ever met a Snorkel Bunny?
They're really very sweet.

They are cuddly, cute, the best kind of friends,
and they have rocket-powered feet!

The Snorkel Bunnies love the sea and work
hard to protect it.

Each plant and creature living there
needs to be respected!

You can find treasures every day when
walking on the beach.

Like sea glass, drift wood, and tiny crabs
whose shells are shiny peach.

But sometimes there are yucky things like
trash and stuff that stinks.

These things can hurt animals – it's worse
than you may think!

3

The Snorkel Bunnies work hard
to clean the beaches every day.

It makes the shore a safer place for all of us
to play!

Now, who are these Snorkel Bunnies
and just what do they do?

To find out, read along with me. Have I got
a story for you!

The oldest Snorkel Bunnies are twins,
Noo-Noo and Little Mo.

They look just alike, love to play games,
and are always on the go!

Rachel Ann is the middle sister, who
happens to be very smart.

She takes photographs all the time and
is very good at art.

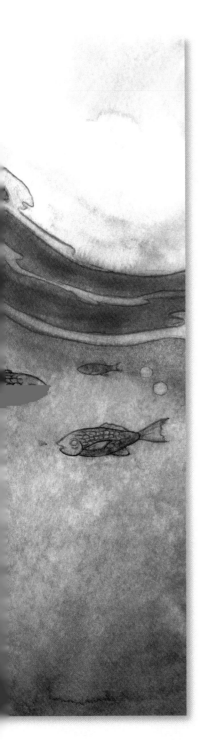

Baby Sami is the youngest and has big blue bunny eyes.

She carries her blanket everywhere and giggles all the time.

She's a Snorkel Bunny in training, just learning what to do.

Her sisters teach how to protect the beach so it's safe for all to use.

Snorkel Bunnies love to swim using their rocket-powered feet.

It propels them fast from place to place, wherever there's a need.

The Bunnies know keeping beaches clean is always right to do.

But following the rules where sea creatures are concerned is very important, too!

Walking home one starry night, it was almost time for bed,

The Bunnies met a mama sea turtle who had just laid her eggs.

She'd dug a nest high in the sand, safe upon the shore.

She worked very hard for over two hours! It really was a chore!

The mama was worried about her babies. Would they make it across the sand?

Creatures who might disturb the nest were always close at hand.

Smiling at the mama, the Bunnies knew what their next job would be.

They'd watch over the nest, and get those hatchlings to the sea.

9

For 60 days and nights, the bunnies watched over the little nest.

Baby Sami got so sleepy, but she really tried her best.

Rachel Ann told those who passed to look but please don't touch.

Turtle eggs are delicate, just looking is enough.

Noo-Noo and Little Mo put up a tiny fence.

That way visitors who came along would know there was a nest.

The bunnies taught about sea turtles to those who stopped to ask.

Protecting this endangered species is a very important task!

The time had come, one moonlit night, the babies began to hatch!

The turtles began their journey across the sand and to the sea at last.

Rachel Ann took lots of pictures. Little Mo and Noo-Noo were very proud.

Baby Sami was full of giggles, and bouncing up and down!

But along came some hungry sea gulls, looking for a treat!

It was then the Snorkel Bunnies used their rocket-powered feet.

They blasted rocket-powered air at the birds up in the sky.

It scared the silly sea gulls and the birds flew right on by!

Because the bunnies protected the eggs by leaving them alone,

The tiny baby sea turtles made it safely to their ocean home!

The hatchlings thanked the sisters before they swam away.

The Snorkel Bunnies waved goodbye. It had been a happy day!

Like the Snorkel Bunnies, you can save endangered sea turtles, too.

There are many things that can hurt them. But here is what you can do.

Always throw your trash away and any you may find.

If sea turtles eat or get trapped by it, they're really in a bind!

And should you see a sea turtle nest when visiting the beach,

Look all you want but never touch! It's the first rule the Bunnies teach.

There are lots of people who work to save sea turtles along our coasts.

They know our help is what these special creatures really need the most!

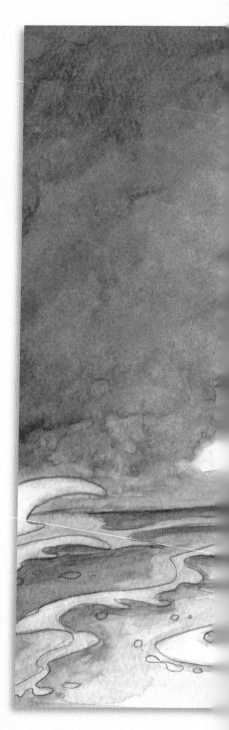

The Snorkel Bunnies protect our beaches – it's an important thing to do.

Now keeping beach creatures safe can be a job for you!

If we all work hard to clean the sea shore each and every day,

Maybe others will do the same – it's the Snorkel Bunny way!

About the Author

Dawn Stanford Calisto grew up in Springfield, VA and is a 1988 graduate from East Carolina University- Special Education major. She is a military spouse and the mother of four daughters. Dawn owns a small business creating sculptures with the treasures she hand picks from the beaches of South Eastern North Carolina and substitutes at a local high school . She shares her love of the seashore and the creatures that reside there through her artwork and writing. Dawn and her husband, COL (R) Joseph Calisto reside with their Golden Retriever, Tucker, at their home in Ocean Isle Beach, NC.

CPSIA information can be obtained at www.ICGtesting.com
Printed in the USA
LVIW01n1211271017
553756LV00001B/2